The Witness

@ COPYRIGHT 2024

BY Antoine Santiago
C/O IMPRESSUM-SERVICE VALLEETSY
PADRE BURGOS AVE,
1000 METRO MANILA

valleetsy-boutique.company.site

DON'T WAIT!
SCAN THE CODE AND
START YOR JOURNEY

GET MORE INFORMATION
VALLEETSY-BOUTIQUE.COMPANY.SITE

This book is only for those who have the courage to explore the boundaries of crime and solve the case.

First things first

Crime novels have their origins in the 19th century and experienced a surge, especially with authors like Edgar Allan Poe. One of the most well-known and influential figures is Sherlock Holmes, created by Sir Arthur Conan Doyle. The golden age of crime fiction spanned the 1920s and 1930s, during which authors like Agatha Christie and Raymond Chandler penned many famous works. Crime novels encompass a variety of subgenres, including detective stories, thrillers, and police procedural novels. They often touch on social and political themes such as corruption and injustice. Popular worldwide, they have developed their own traditions in different countries, from Scandinavian crime fiction to Japanese "Tantei" (detective) stories. Many successful films and TV series are based on crime novels, and they are among the best-selling books worldwide. The genre has produced a multitude of talented authors who have diversified it by bringing in different perspectives and voices.

The witness

Chapter 1

It was a warm summer night, a Friday evening in August. Even though the sun had already set a few hours ago, there was still a pleasant warmth throughout the city. Anna sat alone at the old, remote freight yard and was lost in thought. All the stress that had been going on at her house for a few weeks was slowly but surely becoming unbearable. Her parents just shouted at each other and there was no normal conversation at all anymore. Anna was pretty sure that it probably wouldn't be long before the two finally separated. Well, maybe it was better that way.

She pushed the sleeve of her jacket aside and looked at the clock. It was already a quarter past one, but somehow she didn't feel the need to head home yet. She listened to the noises around her, the usual traffic noise could be heard in the distance, even at night there was still a lot of activity on the streets, but that was probably what big cities had.

In addition to the traffic noise, sirens could now also be heard, perhaps the police or fire department or perhaps just ambulances on the way to an emergency location.

Anna looked around. Apart from a few old railway carriages that increasingly disappeared between the grass, weeds and bushes, there was really nothing special here, but at least here she had peace and quiet. She dug into her bag and pulled out a crumpled box of Marlboros. She took the last cigarette, crushed the empty box in her hand and dropped it next to her.

She then lit the cigarette and took a deep drag. She had often thought about quitting smoking and tried for a while, but in the end the will was too weak. While she inhaled the smoke with pleasure, she thought about what she should tell her mother about why she came home so late, but then she spontaneously thought of something.

When almost only the filter remained of the cigarette, she took one last drag and then flicked it into the dark night. Somehow it was a bit scary here and actually not entirely safe, because there were occasionally homeless people hanging around here looking for a place to sleep or some youth gangs looking for an undisturbed place for their parties.

Anna stood up, brushed the dust off her pants and picked up her bag. She was about to leave when she heard voices a little further away, most likely coming from the other end of the completely dilapidated building she was standing in front of.

The voices grew louder, apparently getting closer. Although the whole thing was a little scary, curiosity finally got the better of her and she would just take a quick look. Anna climbed the dilapidated stairs of the old platform and slowly walked around the building, whose walls were already missing some stones and there were broken roof tiles everywhere, so she had to be careful not to make any noise.

She carefully crept along the wall so as not to be seen. She was only a few steps away from the corner of the house, from there she would definitely be able to see what was going on. At first she only risked a very brief glance. About 150 m away from her there were 6 boys standing on the overgrown train tracks.

The guys were estimated to be 17-20 years old, Anna couldn't tell exactly from the distance.

One of the boys spoke in a rather loud, commanding tone, apparently the boss or leader of the troupe. She had almost lost interest in the whole thing when the so-called "Boss" started to insult one of the boys quite violently, pushing him and then slapping him in the face. The shouting got louder and the group came a little closer to Anna. She took a step back to make sure no one noticed her and tried to listen more closely to what the obvious argument was about.

But unfortunately she only heard fragments and scraps of words. "You're going to betray us all," someone said excitedly. "We're all going to jail because of you," another shouted. "You'll pay for that." Anna suspected that the whole thing must have been pretty serious, but what happened next was a little too blatant for her to have in her life expected.

The boss, who she could now faintly see in the darkness was quite large and strong, walked closer and closer to the guy he had previously pushed and hit. This guy, in turn, a short and rather lanky guy with blonde hair that was visible even in the dark, kept backing away. Suddenly they both stopped abruptly, there was more shouting, but this time Anna couldn't understand a word.

Then the unthinkable happened. The "boss" reached into his inside jacket pocket and pulled out a weapon, some kind of pistol. "Are you afraid?" he asked mockingly. He waved it around and finally held it to his victim's neck. "Do you think I'm afraid of you, you bum? The cops will get you either way." Two of the guys standing around kept looking around nervously. Anna's heart almost stopped, she crouched down and leaned against the wall, otherwise she would probably have fallen over on the spot. She couldn't believe what was happening, it couldn't all be happening. "What am I fucking doing here?" asks! them themselves.

However, the end of all the evil had not yet been reached. Anna had only closed her eyes for a few seconds to make sure it wasn't all just a bad dream, but when a shot rang out out of nowhere, breaking the silence of the night for a moment, she knew it wasn't was a dream, but a harsh reality. The silence returned and there was dead silence in the truest sense of the word. Anna glanced around the corner and quickly put her hands over her face to suppress a scream.

She looked a second time and realized with horror that she had just witnessed a murder. She saw a motionless body lying on the floor, the other guys were just standing there, almost as if what had happened was something completely normal.

Tears welled up in Anna's eyes and ran down her face, the salty drops collected on her lips, and suddenly a feeling of nausea arose within her. The disgusting taste slowly reached her throat and she staggered back a few steps, could no longer hold back and had to vomit. She didn't really feel any better after that, but in this situation that was hardly surprising.

After she had regained some composure, she looked around the corner one more time. The boys were probably having a heated discussion, at least everyone was talking loudly at one another, but Anna couldn't quite understand what was going on. A slightly taller guy with short, dark hair who also seemed to be a bit more muscular had positioned himself in front of the guy with the gun.

It almost looked as if another argument was about to develop. Suddenly the dark-haired man received a punch in the face and then several punches and kicks in the stomach until he finally fell to the ground. But even when he could no longer defend himself, his opponent still gave him a violent kick in the face. Then he said something that Anna could understand for a change, but by now she didn't really care. "If you don't shut up, boy, the same thing will happen to you." The guy on the ground writhed in pain. Shortly afterwards the group broke up, everyone disappeared in other directions, they kept nervously looking around for possible witnesses until finally no one could be seen anymore.

Anna thought about her current situation for a moment and decided that it would be best to get away as quickly as possible. She turned around and unintentionally kicked a roof tile, which then flew into the wall and shattered into its individual pieces with a loud clatter. Panic rose in her, she looked back again and was horrified to see that the injured stranger had noticed her.

Without a second thought, she ran off, down the stairs, through the tall grass, the overgrown tracks, across the entire area. She felt her heart beating wildly in her chest, her fitness was slowly fading, but she couldn't stand still under any circumstances. She glanced over her shoulder and saw that she was being followed, he was pretty fast despite his injuries and was getting closer and closer. She was already looking at the exit gate when fate intervened again.

She tripped over a branch and fell. She had no chance to get up again, she turned onto her back as her pursuer pounced on her and covered her mouth. Anna panicked even more, she lashed out and tried everything to defend herself, but it seemed hopeless, the guy was simply stronger. As he knelt over her, still covering her mouth, she tried to make out his face in the darkness. It took a moment, but she finally recognized him.

The other guy had beaten him up pretty badly, his whole face was covered in blood, but Anna still knew who she was looking at.

Chapter 2

She didn't know his name, but she knew 100 percent that he went to her school, in her parallel class. Still, she had absolutely no idea how to assess him. What if he was a brutal thug and was now turning her over to his buddies? A thousand thoughts ran through her head. Suddenly he spoke to her. "Watch out, I'm taking my hands away from your mouth now, but only if you keep your mouth shut and don't scream, understand?" She nodded and slowly lowered his hands.

"Damn, what the hell are you doing here?"

His voice sounded anything but aggressive, she was calm and understanding, but Anna couldn't quickly find an answer to the question. He sat down next to her, but didn't take his eyes off her for a second. She knew that running away would have been pointless, so she tried to stay calm for now.

Unfortunately that didn't really work, tears welled up in her eyes and she started crying again, she just couldn't help it, what had happened in the last half hour was simply too much for her. The guy put an arm around her shoulder, apparently he really wasn't as brutal an asshole as his friends, but Anna remained suspicious.

"Hey, I won't hurt you, I swear to you."

It took a while until she calmed down a bit, then she looked him directly in the eyes for a moment. "Will you tell me your name?" she avoided his gaze and thought for a moment before answering him.

"So you can rat me out to your friends?"
"Nonsense, why would I do that?"

"Because I saw what you did, you killed someone."

He crossed his hands in front of his face for a moment. "Are you going to turn me in to the cops?" His eyes seemed a little frightened. "No, I don't really know who you are after all." "Nick." He held out his hand and waited for her reaction. She thought for a moment and then took his hand. "I'm Anna." Suddenly voices could be heard again, Anna started to panic, had the guys come back a bit? The two looked around and finally saw a homeless man with his dog a few meters away. Nick jumped up and took Anna by the hand.

"We have to get out of here immediately."

He ran and pulled her behind him, the two of them ran until they reached a subway station, completely out of breath. Anna looked at him fearfully. "And what are we doing now?

The guy saw us and it's probably only a matter of time before he..." She stopped in the middle of her sentence, it would probably be better if she didn't talk about the whole thing in public, even though the platform was deserted. Nick sat down on one of the benches standing around, his face looked even worse in the light. Anna sat down next to him.

"That guy got you pretty bad. Looks really bad." "Not so bad." "And what's next?" "I have no idea." "I have to go home first, after all it's just before three. Or are you planning to keep me here longer?"

He shook his head.

"No, but we'll meet tomorrow, maybe then I'll think of something about what to do next."

"Okay, when and where?" "At 11 a.m. at the Kölnerstrasse sports field." "Okay, see you then."

Commissioner Alexa Peters was still sitting at her desk in the office around half past three in the morning. The coffee in the large, red cup was now cold. She had been sitting in the same place for hours, leafing through countless files. She was slowly getting so tired that her eyes were occasionally starting to close. They were torn from their thoughts when their colleague Thomas Lennart appeared in their office door. In contrast to her, he looked quite rested and gave her one of his usual grins. "Well, you never finish work, do you?"

She gave him a quick look and then ran her hands through her face. "I'm still busy with this drug dealer thing, but somehow I just can't get any further." "You should get some sleep first, maybe then you'll be able to think normally again." "Yes, you're right, I think I'll give myself a few hours ." The conversation between the two was interrupted by Alexa's phone ringing. She walked around the desk, slumped into the chair and finally picked up the phone. "Peters," she answered in a tired voice.

A colleague from the patrol service was speaking on the other end, he seemed quite excited. Lennart watched his colleague concentrate on her telephone conversation and waited for her to hang up. A few minutes later she did the same, but looked anything but pleased. "Well, it seems like my bed still has to wait." "What happened?" "A dead teenager at the freight yard.

Shot in the chest, suicide out of the question." "Okay, I'll drive you there." "You definitely have other things to do." "Yes, but in your condition I definitely won't let you drive." There would have been no point in discussing it here, Alexa took her jeans jacket from the coat rack and followed Lennart into the parking lot. The two got into a 5 Series BMW, which Lennart then drove onto the road towards the freight station. After just 10 minutes they had reached their destination.

There were patrol officers everywhere, as well as lots of press people. The two got out and walked under the police cordon. A colleague arrived immediately, also in civilian clothes, and seemed to be completely out of breath. "Commissioner Peters?

My name is Paul Koch, Homicide Department South, we're already expecting you." Alexa immediately recognized that this was a newcomer who was probably fresh out of police school, so she didn't pay him any attention and continued towards the crime scene. In the distance she saw a familiar face from forensics and made a detour there.

"Hello Klaus, what do you have?"

"Oh, I haven't seen Alexa for a long time, unfortunately not too much so far.

As you probably know, the boy was killed by a shot in the chest, clearly murder, the type of weapon is still being checked. We have cigarette butts,a few bottles but that's about it. Oh yes, and the fingerprints on the corpse still have to be checked." "Well, that's better than nothing, thank you.

" She turned back to Lennart and continued with him to the corpse. The boy lay there as he was found, pale and staring blankly at the sky. Another police officer approached Alexa. "Hello Ms. Peters, it looks like it's going to be another long night for you." "Yes, you can say that. Could you already identify the boy?"

"However, he had a wallet with him with ID and everything. His name is Phillip Schubert, 17 years old.

According to his student ID, he was a student at Morgenstern Comprehensive School. We don't know more yet, we're just trying to reach the parents." "Who found him?" "A homeless man, he says he was looking for a place to sleep with his dog." "Any other witnesses?"

"Not directly, the man says he saw two young people running away from a distance, a boy and a girl with blonde hair. However, I have to say that the man smells like a whole liquor distillery, which of course doesn't mean anything. Well, I have to move on if you don't have any further questions?"

"No, not thanks for the moment." Alexa saw the boy's body being transported away , she looked around for a moment and then asked her colleague Lennart to leave.

There was silence on the way back to the office. Somehow this boy seemed familiar to the inspector, but at the moment she didn't know exactly where to put him.

When they got back to the police station parking lot it was just after five.

Alexa felt every muscle and bone in her body, so she quickly decided that it would be better to sleep for a few hours first.

Chapter 3

Just before eleven the next day, Nick reached the sports field where he had arranged to meet Anna. She didn't seem to be there yet, so he sat down on a bench and lit a cigarette. He kept looking around nervously, if one of his people saw him with Anna, both of them might make their will. The gash above his right eye, which he had patched up with a makeshift plaster, still hurt like hell. After he finished smoking, he pulled his cell phone out of his pocket; there was still no sign of Anna at five past eleven.

He became more and more impatient that women could never be on time. When he finally got up to look around again, she finally appeared.

She seemed quite out of breath. "Sorry, but I missed the subway and since I unfortunately don't have telepathic abilities, I couldn't tell you that." "It's okay." Anna looked at him for a moment without saying anything, the matter seemed pretty good to finish, at least that's what it looked like to her. "Have you been to the doctor?"

She points to his head injury. "For what reason? It's not that bad, it just hurts a little, but it'll be okay." "Well, if you say so." He was quite stubborn, that was clear and it was clear to her that she couldn't convince him to see a doctor anyway to get it checked out, so she didn't even try. "And have you thought about what to do next?"

She pulled a piece of paper out of her pocket, a newspaper article. She unfolded the page and handed it to Nick.

It was the front page of the daily newspaper and it said in big, bold letters: "Dead at the freight yard, teenager killed by gun." Nick skimmed through the article and at the end asked the police that any witnesses should definitely come forward immediately. "Shit."

"You can probably say that out loud." He sat back down on the bench, rested his arms on his knees and held his face with his hands. Anna sat down next to him and waited for a reaction. When there was nothing but silence for a long time, she spoke up.

"Are you telling me why all this happened?" He sat up straight again and lit a cigarette.

After he took a deep drag, the answer finally came. "If I tell you this now, you'll be just as deeply involved in the whole thing as I am." "Don't I already? Nick, I saw the murder and didn't sleep all night because I kept thinking about why the guy had to die. So now please tell me what's going on.

" Her voice sounded assertive and Nick realized that there was no point in giving her any excuses. "

Yes, okay. But you swear to me that it will remain our secret?" "Of course, I promise." "Watch out, the guys I was there with last night work for a drug lord,"A pretty brutal one to be honest, as well." Anna looked at him, stunned and confused. "You're a junkie?"

"No, you're crazy, let me finish first. So this drug lord regularly receives deliveries of all kinds of drugs, coke, heroin, speed, etc.

The stuff comes from Colombia and elsewhere. Well, in any case, we have to see that the drugs come from the port directly to all of his dealers and collect money for them. When things go well, sometimes you get €500 a day and when things go badly, he sends his thugs after you." Anna looked at him in complete shock. "Why are you doing this, Nick? Do you take that kind of shit too?" He saw the disappointment in her eyes. "Hey, I swear to you that I won't tackle this stuff."

"Then why?" "I ran away from home two months ago because I was under extreme stress, I live with a friend and I just need money to finally get something to search for your own. One of the guys who takes part goes to my class and said that you get a lot of money there.

Then I thought I'd do it for a few weeks until I had enough money and then I'd get out again, but it's not that easy." "And then what happened last night?" "Phillip, the guy she I've only been there for a short time and of course I immediately checked what kind of lousy business was going on. It was all far too risky for him and he wanted to get out again. So the boss said we should scare him a little and get him to stick with it.

Phillip then started provoking Richie, the guy with the gun, he said he wanted to go to the cops and put us all in jail. Well, then Richie completely freaked out and shot him." "And now what do you want to do? Pretend none of this happened?" He stood up and turned his back on her.

"No damn, I don't know what to do, if I go to the cops they'll call me out too, they don't know anything about it."

Anna got up, went to him and took him in her arms. It took a moment but then Nick returned the hug. Even though she barely knew him, she was suddenly quite afraid for him. They just stood there for a while, Anna felt a little safer around Nick, but she knew that if the guys found out what she had seen, she would be in a lot of danger, because apparently these people really had no scruples. She pulled away from the hug and looked at Nick with a serious look. "I'm scared."

"They won't hurt you, they don't know what you saw." "And what about you?" "Well, we'll see." He looked at the clock again, it was now close to time twelve. He had to be seen by the boys again. "I have to go, otherwise they'll think I was with the cops." "Take care of yourself."

" I promise.He was about to turn around to leave when Anna held back for a moment. "Nick?" He looked at her and saw that she was quite worried. "Can I call you if something happens?" "Sure." She dug her cell phone out of her pocket and Nick took a few steps towards her. He saved his number on and then asked for hers. Then he said his final goodbye and left. Anna watched him go for a while before setting off herself. She really hoped that she hadn't seen the last of him.

Meanwhile, the young clique around Mike, Steve, Alex and Richie sat in their so-called headquarters, an old, run-down warehouse at the harbor. It had been empty for many years and was now used by boys as a meeting place.

The building was already quite dilapidated, so an outsider would never have guessed that anyone was there. Even though it was only midday, a bottle of vodka was already making the rounds. Suddenly the door was pushed open with a loud bang and a huge guy with a bouncer's build and a leather jacket entered the room. He really was quite the muscle, you shouldn't meet someone like him alone in the dark.

He had a fairly large scar on his right cheek that most likely came from a knife. The boys stopped their ceremony and all looked at him with wide eyes in awe. He glanced at Richie and twisted his face into a devious grin. "Richie, I think the two of us have something important to talk about. In private."

He turned around and left the room, his shoes clattering loudly on the wooden floor. Richie took one last long drink from the vodka bottle and then followed him. The guy, who everyone just called Lupo, was known in real life as Ludger Müller.

He had moved into one of the side rooms and was waiting for the person he was talking to. He had sat down in an old armchair and crossed his legs when Richie entered. "Please close the door," he said firmly. Richie did as he was told and took a few steps closer.

"What's up?" Lupo stood up, gold bracelets rattled on his wrist, he walked up and down in front of one of the dirty windows, the clacking of his shoes made Richie extremely nervous. "I thought you were going to explain to me what was going on," he said in a mocking tone.

He pulled a newspaper out of his inside jacket pocket and threw it onto a small, rickety wooden table that stood next to the armchair. "Look at this." Richie walked slowly and uncertainly towards the table; he could see the front page of the daily newspaper from a little distance away. Lupo went to him, grabbed him by the neck with a tight grip and slammed his face on the table, causing it to break apart. Richie felt blood pooling in his mouth and nose and eventually running down his face.

"Can you explain this shit to me, you complete idiot. Now don't give me any stupid excuses."

His tone was angry and filled with hatred, you could practically see how the anger was rising more and more within him. "So I… well…" Richie stammered.

Lupo picked up the newspaper and read out: "Dead at the freight yard, teenager killed by gun, 17-year-old Phillip S. and so on, and so on..." Richie was still kneeling in front of the now broken table,Lupo jerked him back to his feet and gave him a hard slap in the face.

He staggered back a little, one hand holding his cheek, which was throbbing with pain. "You should scare him, warn him, but don't fucking kill him." He was beside himself with anger and kicked the old chair, which then also shattered into all its pieces with a clatter. "Phillip provoked me, he said he was going to the cops."

"Listen, you little bum, if I killed everyone who provoked me straight away, this town wouldn't have many inhabitants anymore. Where is Nick anyway?" Richie was visibly intimidated.

"Well, he interfered and wanted to ruin my performance, so I gave him a few punches." Lupo's eyes practically glowed with hatred and anger. He walked up to Richie and kicked him in the stomach. He doubled over in pain. "Now pay attention, you miserable loser don't have anything to report here that I didn't order, is that clear?

Nick is one of our best people and he definitely wouldn't have made such a shitty mistake, so just be careful what you do next and don't you dare touch Nick again or I might forget myself. Did that get into your little brain?" "Yeah, okay, I got it," Richie stammered. "I hope so for you, just pull yourself together." Lupo left the room and Richie was left alone.

He thought for a moment. He couldn't possibly show himself like that in front of his people. He stood up slowly, his face and stomach still hurting, then he walked quietly across the hallway so as not to draw attention to himself and disappeared.Did that get into your little brain?" "Yeah, okay, I got it," Richie stammered. "I hope so for you, just pull yourself together." Lupo left the room and Richie was left alone. He thought for a moment.

He couldn't possibly show himself like that in front of his people. He stood up slowly, his face and stomach still hurting, then he walked quietly across the hallway so as not to draw attention to himself and disappeared.Did that get into your little brain?" "Yeah, okay, I got it," Richie stammered. "I hope so for you, just pull yourself together." Lupo left the room and Richie was left alone.

He thought for a moment. He couldn't possibly show himself like that in front of his people. He stood up slowly, his face and stomach still hurting, then he walked quietly across the hallway so as not to draw attention to himself and disappeared.

When Nick arrived at his gang at the harbor around half past twelve, the boys were still sitting with their bottles of vodka. "Oh, there's one for you too," he was greeted by Steve. "Sure, but not everyone can drink a bottle of vodka for breakfast." "Lupo was just here and was really stressed out. I think Richie got a few punches in the mouth." "Well, I think it's his own fault."

Chapter 4

While the boys continued their conversation in a happy atmosphere, Inspector Peters woke up from her deep sleep in her apartment. It had actually been more of a long nightmare. The whole time she had had the image of the murdered boy in her head, she was quite sure that he looked quite familiar, she just didn't quite know where from. After thinking about it for a moment, she slowly crawled out of her bed and jumped into the shower. As the water ran down her body, the brilliant thought suddenly occurred to her.

She finished her personal hygiene in no time, ran to her room wearing only a towel and slipped into dry clothes. She then ran into the kitchen, where she quickly threw a few things into her bag, took the key from the key rack and then left the apartment as quickly as possible.

She rushed down the stairs and almost lost her balance had it not been for the banister. When she stepped outside, she was met with incredible heat. She threw her bag onto the passenger seat of her BMW convertible, opened the roof and got behind the wheel.

On the way to the office she ran three red lights and two stop signs. When she then turned into the police station parking lot at an incredible speed, she almost ran over a colleague, but luckily she was just able to brake.

She parked in her usual parking space, closed the convertible roof and finally made her way to her office. There was a lot of activity in the hallways, with police officers running back and forth, conducting interviews or dragging someone behind them in handcuffs, so it was business as usual.

Alexa quickly went into the small kitchen to organize some coffee. Once this was done, we got to work. She entered her office and had to open all the windows because of the unbearable heat. She then threw herself into her desk chair and glanced into the next room, where her colleague Lennart was conducting an interrogation.

After observing everything for a moment, she went back to her own business, which was why she came here after all. She rummaged through the files that were scattered across her desk, her mind always on the dead boy from last night. After a few minutes she finally found what she was looking for, a file about a drug bust. She went over one page after the other, looked closely at the names and finally there he was Phillip Schubert.

She looked at the date of the report, it was only 2 weeks old. She leaned back, picked up her coffee cup and took a few sips. A lead had just opened up, maybe she could solve two cases at once, but she would still have a lot of work to do before then.A moment later Lennart walked into the office, sat on the corner of the desk and looked at his colleague. "Well, Mrs. Peters, you probably didn't last long at home." "Well, my dear Thomas, I came across a very interesting clue." "Sounds very exciting, I've just questioned the homeless man.

He swears he saw two people at the crime scene." "Could he describe them?" "Well, he said the girl was blonde and slim and the guy was tall and dark-haired, not much, that could probably be every other person here."

"Okay, so to my news, the boy who was shot, Phillip, was questioned about a drug raid two weeks ago." "Are there any names?" "I just skimmed through the file but I'll get back to it and work through everything again. "Well then have fun, I have to write the minutes first, so see you later." He left his place on the edge of the table and went back into the next room while Alexa turned her attention back to the file, which might still have some useful information for her.

Anna was just on the way home, she and her friend Charline had met in town to chat, she almost let slip what she had experienced the evening before, but then she was just able to hold back and switch to another topic swing around.

Now she was sitting in the subway and thinking about Nick, she looked around, the compartment was pretty crowded, opposite her were two homeless people who were staring at her the whole time. One of the two pulled a cell phone out of his dirty pants pocket, a fairly new model with photo and video functions. She got out at the next station, rummaged in her bag and shortly afterwards lit a cigarette. As she walked along the platform and the subway passed her, the two homeless people were still looking at her.

Then it suddenly dawned on her, she thought back to yesterday's experience and realized that the homeless man on the subway had probably been the one who had surprised you and Nick at the freight yard.

She felt sick and a kind of panic rose up in her again. The guy recognized her, that was for sure, why else would he have stared at her like that the whole time. That couldn't be true, it couldn't be true what if he went to the police.

And... damn the cell phone, he had taken a photo of her, shit, now she was in a lot of trouble, it was probably only a matter of time before the police came after her. She took one last drag from her cigarette and flicked the butt onto the tracks. She then pulled her cell phone out of her pocket and dialed Nick's number.

After the 5th ring the mailbox answered. "Hey Nick, it's me. I really need to talk to you, it's really damn important, please get in touch with me."

She put her cell phone back in her pocket and continued on her way home.

Just as she reached the door, her cell phone rang. It was Nick. "Yes?" "It's Nick. What's so urgent?" "Can we meet, I don't want to discuss this with you on the phone." "Sounds very mysterious.

I'm on my way home right now, if you want you can come by my place." He gave her the address and she agreed. "Okay, see you soon then."

Chapter 5

Alexa and her colleague Lennart were sitting together over the files that contained all the information about the drug scene when suddenly a man stormed into the office. Followed by an angry colleague who tried to stop him.

"I'm sorry, but the gentleman really wanted to speak to you." Alexa recognized him as the homeless man whom Lennart had interrogated a few hours earlier. He seemed pretty excited and was waving a cell phone in his hand. "Mr. Lennart, I have it." Lennart nodded to his colleague who was standing in the doorway and she left the room. "Mr. Huber, who do you have?"

Alexa seemed a little unsure and looked at Thomas incredulously, who winked at her and then turned back to his visitor.

"Well, the girl I told you about, I saw her again, she was sitting in my subway, I took a photo with my cell phone." Inspector Petersen intervened.

"You can't just take pictures of complete strangers without their consent." "Yes, but she was there where I found the dead man." "Show me here.

" Lennart took the cell phone from him and looked at the picture. It showed a young girl, probably around 17-19 years old, with long blonde hair. "And you are really sure that it was her." "Of course, one hundred percent."

"Mr. Huber, it was night when you saw her."

"Yes, but she was wearing this white jacket with such a big, black hooks on the back, just like the ones in the subway." Lennart whispered to Petersen with a grin on his face.

"A Nike jacket, I mean the catch." "Are you going to do something now, arrest her or something?" "Mr. Huber, we'll first try to find her and talk to her and then we'll see. We will confiscate your cell phone first. Maybe it could serve as evidence." "But I need that." "You'll probably be able to get by without it for a few days." He grimaced and muttered something incomprehensible to himself; he seemed quite offended. A few minutes later he disappeared just as quickly as he appeared.

When the two inspectors were among themselves again, they looked again at the two photos of the alleged witness or perhaps suspect. "I would say we question the PC, right?" suggested Lennart.

" Okay, you go over to Kalli with the picture, I'll look at the files again and see if I can find anything about a girl that matches the picture. Maybe she's also in the drug scene." "All right."

Alexa continued to struggle with her files, she was pretty sure that the dead boy had somehow been involved in drug deals. During the raid at the train station he was only caught with a few grams of hash, but she still had a bad feeling about the whole thing, something wasn't right. And sooner or later she would find out what he was, she was sure of it.

Fifteen minutes later Lennart came back cheerfully, grinning. "Bingo Madame." He placed a printout of a photo on Alexa's desk.

"Her name is Anna Berger, she is 17 years old, and so far she has been caught twice for minor shoplifting and in a fight, but only as a friend of the victim at the time, so far she has only been warned and has actually not been guilty of anything major, but At least we know who she is."

"And you're sure she's the right one?" "And as I'm sure." "What if our homeless super spy was wrong, there are probably others who look like that. "

" I'll at least talk to her once, it doesn't cost anything to ask and if we're mistaken, which I don't think we are, then we'll just have to keep looking.” “Well then you know what you have to do. I don't want to wait until we find the next dead person somewhere here." "I'm already on my way, see you later. "Good luck."

Nick was coming out of the bathroom when the doorbell rang. He had showered and was only wearing jeans. He actually wanted to quickly put on a T-shirt, but the doorbell rang again. Since he was of the firm opinion that one of his roommates had forgotten his key again, he went to the apartment door to open it. When Anna stood in front of him, he was a little surprised at first.

“Hey, that was quick, I wasn’t expecting you.” “Am I disturbing you? Sorry, but I really need to talk to you." "Nonsense, you're not bothering me, come in." She entered and he led her through the hallway into the living room.

" Sit down now, I'll just quickly put some clothes on." He left the room again and Anna looked around a little.

The apartment wasn't particularly big, but it was pretty chic in a way, and she could handle it here too. It would be a thousand times better here than with her constantly arguing parents, but she would probably have to endure it for a while. It didn't take long for Nick to come back, he sat down on the sofa opposite her and looked at her for a moment.

"And what's so urgent now?"

Anna glanced around the room.

"You don't live here with these killer types, do you?"

" No, my roommates are really harmless. But you're hardly here to ask me that, are you?" "No, of course not. Nick, that bum who saw us on the train site..."

"What about him?" "I saw him again. "Earlier in the subway." "And?" "He recognized me, damn it, he took a picture of me with his fucking cell phone." "You're not serious, are you? Why didn't you do anything?" "I only realized who he was when I got out and then it was too late anyway."

Nick held his hands in front of his face for a moment before answering. "I hope he doesn't go to the cops now." "And what if he does?" "Well, I think we have a really big problem then." "Man Nick, what should I do now?"

"I have no idea at the moment we can only wait and see I hope the cops don't find out anything." Nick looked in his pocket for cigarettes, because of this shock he urgently had to smoke one.

Finally he pulled out a crumpled pack of Marlboros, lit a cigarette and took a long drag.

There was absolute silence for a while; Anna had also lit a cigarette and was trying to think about what to do next.

The silence was broken when Anna's cell phone rang.

About the Author

Antoine Santiago, a young and emerging author in the realm of crime fiction, brings a fresh perspective to the genre with his gripping narratives and keen insight into the human psyche. Born with a natural gift for storytelling, Santiago weaves intricate plots filled with twists and turns that keep readers on the edge of their seats. His characters are multi-dimensional, flawed yet relatable, drawing readers into their world of mystery and intrigue.

With a penchant for exploring the darker aspects of society, Santiago delves fearlessly into themes of corruption, betrayal, and redemption. His writing is marked by its authenticity, as he draws inspiration from real-life experiences and observations. Each page crackles with tension as Santiago masterfully builds suspense, leading readers down unexpected paths towards startling revelations.

Despite his youth, Santiago's talent has garnered widespread acclaim, earning him a dedicated following of fans eager for each new release. With an ever-growing repertoire of novels that push the boundaries of the genre, Antoine Santiago is poised to leave an indelible mark on the world of crime fiction.

www.ingramcontent.com/pod-product-compliance
Lightning Source LLC
Chambersburg PA
CBHW070919160726
48004CB00003B/1433